DOODLE DANDIES

doodle

poems that

w
o
r
d
s

J. Patrick Lewis

An Anne Schwartz Book
ATHENEUM BOOKS FOR YOUNG READERS

dandies
take shape

images

Lisa Desimini

with design and typography by
Ann Bobco
and
Lisa Desimini

Atheneum Books for Young Readers
An imprint of Simon & Schuster Children's Publishing Division
1230 Avenue of the Americas
New York, New York 10020

Book design by Ann Bobco and Lisa Desimini
The illustrations are rendered in mixed media.
First Edition
Printed in the United States of America
10   9   8   7   6   5   4   3   2   1
Library of Congress Cataloging-in-Publication Data
Lewis, J. Patrick.
Doodle dandies : poems that take shape / by J. Patrick Lewis ;
illustrated by Lisa Desimini. — 1st ed.
Summary: A collection of poems, each of which appears on the page
in the shape of its subject.
ISBN 0-689-81075-X
1. Children's poetry, American. 2. Visual poetry, American.
[1. American poetry. 2. Visual poetry.]
I. Desimini, Lisa, ill. II. Title.
PS3562.E9465D66   1998
811'.54—dc20   96-1920

Thanks to Lee Bennett Hopkins, editor of *Extra Innings*
(Harcourt, Brace & Company, 1993), who first published
"A Swing and a Miss" as "Great Pitches."

"Giraffe" appeared in *Ranger Rick* magazine (December 1994).
"Sky High" and "Winter" appeared in *Storyworks* magazine (January 1995).

Special thanks to Paul Colin.

JUDE

—J. P. L.

FIONA

—L. D.

First Burst of Spring

The day is cold, the earth is mud, but

don't let anything stop you, Bud!

Dachshund

Here comes the lady with the diamond ring
walking a dog like a sausage on a string
there goes the dog with his nose in the air
walking the lady with the purple hair!

giraffe

Tree-tall
giraffe
up
to
his
neck

in brown and yellow
patchwork quilts, turns
and hobbles away
on wooden

tail

stilts   stilts   stilts   stilts

The fastball
that you hope to poke
is smoke

The screwball
an ironic twist
hits your fist

A Swing and a Miss

The knuckler
wobbling up to you
can dipsy-do

The let-up pitch
you can't resist?
you missed

The curveball
that you thought was there
is air

The sinker
comes as some surprise:
it dies

The spitball
that by law's forbidden
(is hidden)

weeping willow

Her wind-woven hair softly sweeping

In
a far
field
of
sad
ness
stands
the
wee
wid
ow
wee
ping

Skinny BONNIE Bumber
wears a long, tall hat. I hide her
in the closet till the clouds get fat. I poke her up
and out when the sun goes away. Fattie Bonnie Bumber

loves a rainy day!

umbrella

The butterfly is

the fantasy fulfiller of every caterpillar

day delights

in jungle cries

BIG
CAT

night ignites
its tiger eyes

synchronized
swim team

A swimming FROM pool UNDER with WATER wrinkled EIGHT

waves is **PRECISION** **NEEDLES** like a **POKING** quilt of **THROUGH** blue

The Oyster Family

An
oyster boy,
an oyster girl,
an oyster dad,
a mother-of-pearl

I slithered down to Pepper Pond for a midnight snack, a picker-upper. I missed a mouse and beetle bug, so I ate a

BULL FROG

for my supper. Well, he was tough as toad, and chewy. Mighty leggy, mighty lumpy. And let me tell you, Creep, I'm feeling mighty Jumpy!

Creep and Slither

winter

when sky unravels its cold mist-eries

fluttering down brown skeletons of trees

these speckles on a page can barely show

the spectacle of unexpected snow

All eyes look down
the
cinder
track—
the
pole
vault
pole
connects,
bends
back . . .
the
boy
who's
hurled
above
the
bar
returns
to
earth
a falling
star.

Sky High

Mirror

You looking out
at me looking in—
I am an I-
dentical twin!
Did I just wink?
I thought I did,
because you flut-
tered your eyelid.
When one of you
makes two of me
there's twice as much
of us to see!

Mirror

You looking out
at me looking in—
I am an I-
dentical twin!
Did I just wink?
I thought I did,
because you flut-
tered your eyelid.
When one of you
makes two of me
there's twice as much
of us to see!

How many humps?

As the number of humps
on a camel goes,
the dromedary is

ordinary

But the number of humps
on a camel grows,
and the bactrian is

extraordinary

Off a

coming

Lashondra's

clock!

On the

seconds left

Only

bl●ck!

She takes a cr●ss-

c●urt pass

from y●u and

banks it off the glass f●r

tw●

LASHONDRA
SCORES!

SKYSCRAPER

I
am
a
nee
dle
of
steel
glass &
cement
1 0 2
s t o r i e s
high on a clear
day you can see
2 0 0
miles out into the
Atlantic or watch
hundreds of ants
scurrying like
people on the sidewalks
below & the yellow
bugs racing recklessly
along the city streets &
ride the elevator all the
way down in 37 seconds
FLAT

The Turtle

is a giant hurdle

I AM
A COSMIC
SNOWBALL MADE
OF DUSTY ICE AND GAS.
ONCE OR TWICE A CENTURY
I PASS THE EARTH AND
SUN. SEE YA NEXT
TIME AROUND . . .
IN 2061!

HALLEY'S COMET